U0931692

Everything in time.

一切及時

b. wing

Everything, in Time

My father passed away last year.
The last thing he said to me was,
"Oh, sis, time goes by so fast."
He thought I was his sister the entire time.

So fast that we forget it,
So fast that we don't use it,
So fast that we mistreat it.

While working on this book,
I learned of Khalil Fong's passing.
I saw the news on Instagram
while I had a mouthful of rice.
Is there a place that cradles the souls of the departed?
I imagine a gathering of untethered souls,
chatting as if there's no tomorrow.
Every moment in this life and in this body is unique.
It's never about the big things; it's about the simplest seconds
that make us smile, make us cry, make us swear, and give us butterflies.

You opened the door and beheld your newborn child.
A sip of beer at the finish line.
The rain tapping against the window.
The warmth of the sun on your skin.
The sound of laughter Fingers poised on piano keys,

(The Clock is Ticking)

ready to play the first note.
The unfolding of a flower's petals.
A deep breath before sunrise.
A glance back after saying goodbye.
Finally, I held your hand.
The sharp sting of a burned finger.
The timer is up.
The kitten squinting as it peeks into your bed...
Your classmate leaped into the water,
splashing everyone.
Yawning together.
Pouring water over the coffee beans.
Catching the very first glimpse of a rainbow.
The thrill of soaring into the air on a trampoline.
Realizing your parents aren't
as strong as they once were.
The moment I understood my dream has shattered.

I believe memories
aren't just locked away in our minds;
they're scattered throughout our bodies,
like little snakes,
ready to strike when you least expect it.
It can be painful, and I still bury my face in my hands
out of embarrassment sometime when I look back.

At the end of the day,
I want to leave this world with a heart that is worn out
and tender like medium rare steak,
aching from battles fought,
yet still preserving and striving for the best.
I tried, I risked, I turned every loss into a lesson,
and I'm proud of the person I've become.

Welcome to "THE" moment.

一切，及時

我的父親去年年尾去世了。
他對我說的最後一句話是：
「哦，妹，時光過得真快。」
那段日子，他一直以為我是他的妹妹。

快到我們忘記了，
快到我們漠視它，
快到我們欺負它。

在寫這本書的時候，
我從 Instagram 看見方大同過世的消息。
當時我一口都是飯。
那個存放靈魂的地方，現在會不會有點兒擠迫？
我想像一群靈魂聚集在一起輕輕無言地混沌着。

此生此身中的每一刻都是獨一無二的。
大概都與大事無關；是那幾秒鐘，
讓我們微笑，讓我們哭泣，讓我們咒罵，
讓我們心裡小鹿亂撞的一瞬間。

你打開門，看到了你剛出生的孩子。
在終點線喝一口啤酒。
雨點敲打著窗戶。
陽光照在你肌膚上的溫暖。
笑聲。
手指放在鋼琴鍵上，準備彈奏第一個音符。
花瓣綻放。

（時鐘在滴答滴答）

日出前呼一口氣。
告別後再回首一眼。
終於，我握住了你的手。
手指燒傷時的刺痛。
計時器響起。
小貓瞇著眼睛偷看你的床……
同學跳入水裡，濺了大家一身水。
在課室中一起打哈欠。
將水倒在磨研了的咖啡豆上。
看見彩虹。
跳彈床彈在半空。
突然意識到父母不再像以前那麼堅壯。
當我明白我的夢想破滅的時候。

我相信記憶不僅被鎖在我們的大腦裡；
它們就像小蛇一樣遍佈我們全身，
準備在你最意想不到的時候發動攻擊。
會痛苦的。回首往事，我仍然會尷尬到雙手掩臉。

希望自己到了最後，離開這個世界時，
心即使疲憊不堪，卻又溫柔軟熟如五分熟牛排。
經歷這許多，心裡卻依然保留著最好的，並為之奮鬥。
我嘗試過，我冒險過，我成功過，
我把每一次的失敗都當成一次教訓，
我興幸自己成為這樣的人。

歡迎來到「此刻」。

01

"I'm still waiting to hand you the party hat."

You make me happy, it also means you can make me very very sad and that worries me, frankly.

「我還在等著把派對帽遞給你。」
你讓我快樂，這也意味著你會讓我非常非常悲傷，
坦白說，這讓我擔心。

wing

02

Tranquility | 寧靜

I like to imagine myself as a giant squid changing colors, waiting in the deep sea to greet you.

我喜歡把自己想像成一隻變色的巨型烏賊，
在深海裡等著迎接你。

FamilyMart
ATM

03

I'm up here contemplating my life. Again. Yay.

我在這裡思考我的人生。再一次。耶。

04

The moment you laugh alone and hear the echo and you like it, you will be okay.

當你獨自一人笑着，聽到迴聲，並且喜歡它的時候，你就沒事了。

05

I discover a cloud floating by and wonder if I've accidentally walked to heaven.

我發現一朵雲飄過，我是否不小心走到了天堂。

06

In the sky (should be like this?)

在天空上（應該是這樣子的？）

07

See you on the next wave, shall we eat together next time?

下波見，下次一起吃飯好嗎？

08

Hey guys, breakfast is over,
time for mediation! Time for meditation!

嘿，早餐結束了，冥想時間到了！
冥想時間到了！（私人冥想團）

09

Time to go home, myself, my star and the sound of the forest.

是時候回家了，我自己，我的星星和森林的聲音。

10

Everything is not under our control. Where are you rushing to?

一切都不在我們的掌控之中。你急著去哪裡？

11

When you felt sad, did you ever draw a deep cave and confess to it?

傷心的時候有沒有畫過深深的洞穴對着他傾吐呢？

12

Emergency hug in progress. Sorry for the inconvenience.

緊急繾綣中，造成不便敬請原諒。

13

Dear God, I want to say, we are not bad people. But, we did a few bad things. Is that ok? Are we still going to heaven?

親愛的上帝，我想說，我們不是壞人。但是，我們做了一些壞事。可以嗎？我們還會上天堂嗎？

14

Who are you when no one is looking? I like to fly around.

當沒人注意的時候你是誰？我喜歡飛來飛去。

15

I love to breathe out white mist on a very cold day,
pretending to smoke.
(After spending years waiting alone at the bus station,
pretending to smoke, I considered quitting school.)

好喜歡在很冷很冷的天氣裡口中吐出白氣，
假裝自己在吸煙。
(獨自在荒無人煙的公車站假裝
吸煙了幾年，讓我想退學。)

16

It took me all these years to realize that everything can be said in silence.

這麼多年我才明白一切都可以無聲地說。

17

Many things seem to happen in the park: heartbroken, joy, falling in love, and the first kiss.
(Time stood still then, expanding at a slow rhythm. It seems like a lifetime is very long.)

有許多事情好像都在公園裡發生。受傷，快樂，談戀愛，第一次有人吻你的嘴。
(那時候時間靜止著，凝固在某一點，又以極慢的節奏擴張。好像一生很長的樣子。)

18

I can't keep up with the beat —— my heartbeat, dance beat, song beat —— any beat. But I promise you, this soul is fun; are you ready for my performance?

我跟不上節奏 —— 我的心跳、舞蹈節奏、歌曲節奏 —— 任何節奏。
但我向你保證，這個靈魂很有趣；你準備好觀賞我的表演了嗎？

19

Why are you being so nice to me?

為什麼對我這麼好？

20

The voices in my head, to be honest, are not very good speakers.

說實話，我腦子裡的聲音甚至比我更不會說話。

21

I am hiding here, waiting for the flowers to bloom.

等花開等花開等花開。

22

If it is not weird, I am not interested.

如果它不夠奇怪，我沒興趣。

23

“Lord I’m doing all I can, to be a better man”

After practicing my superpowers, I’m not sure if the apple is still edible. If yes, I'll try watermelon next time.

"Lord I'm doing all I can, to be a better man"
在我施展超能力之後，我不確定這個蘋果是否還能吃。
如果可以，下次我試試西瓜。

24

Do I look like this?

我看起來是這樣嗎？

25

I missed you quietly today, so quietly that no one noticed.
But I felt it like rock and roll inside me.

今天靜靜地想你，靜靜地，沒有人注意到。
心裡面是燒焦，灼熱，搖滾。

26

Not really, I am not quiet. I ran out of things to say.

不，我不安靜。已經沒什麼好說的。

27

Would you come by to see me?
I will pretend I'm sleeping.

你會來找我嗎？我會一直裝睡。

I haven't met all of me yet.

我還沒見過全部的自己。

29

Shhh...remember, when you see it, you must act as if you do not see it. If you gossip, it will stay and listen.

噓……你必須假裝沒看見。如果你在說八卦，它會留下來聽。

30

Even if it's only for 5 seconds. That's enough.

哪怕只有 5 秒。也夠了。

31

Wind Tasting | 食風

I used to think every day about how to run away from home; now I'm just thinking about how to get home sooner.

我以前每一天都在想如何離家出走，現在卻想着如何早啲返屋企。

32

Don't think you can go anywhere while I'm staring at you hard with my mental power.
用嚟念力望實你。睇吓你走去邊。

33

Sometimes, it feels like the air is so thin that it's like living in outer space.

有時，感覺空氣非常稀薄，就像活在外太空一樣。

34

Really? Really.

真的？真的。

35

Shall we play "Look, Look"? The first person to laugh or fail to do so loses. Sounds good?

我們玩「鬥望」好嗎？誰先笑誰輸。好不好？

36

I will sink your words to the bottom of my heart until I can no longer see them.

我會將你的話下沉到心的最底部，直到再也看不見它們。

Our last goodbye was never said

37

Our last goodbye was never said.

我們未說最後的再見。

38

I imagine myself as a big shot for ten minutes each day.
After a bit of giggling and singing. I begin my work.

每天我花十分鐘在這裡幻想自己叱咤風雲，偷笑完唱埋首飲歌就會開始工作。

39

We are very much down to earth, just not this earth.

（這句沒有中文版，翻譯不來。）

40

"The Necessity of a Smiley Face" |「笑容的必要性」

It's scientifically proven that faking a smile tricks your brain into believing you are happy.

(May I ask who the scientist is?)

科學證明，假笑可以欺騙你的大腦，讓它相信你是快樂的。
（請問那位科學家是誰？）

41

As I step onto the quiet street at night,
It feels as if I'm walking on the moon,
fully embracing the silence that surrounds me.

That is freedom.
and it is free.

踏上夜晚安靜的街道時，
感覺就像在月球上散步。
可以浮沉於周圍的寂靜。

這是自由。
免費的。

42

Sometimes, I would rather be that fox.

有時候我寧願是那隻狐狸。

43

I’m serious about this: I really don’t like squashed cakes and breads.

我是認真的，我不喜歡壓扁了的蛋糕和麵包。

44

It was an unimaginable summer.

那是一個不可思議的夏。

45

It's a colorful sky.

天空多姿多彩。

Small reminders

A notes for myself
and for anyone else who finds it relevant:

Always take care of your health.
We have one life, and we may not get another.
You just have to keep going,
give this life the chance to become your masterpiece.

It's hard—it's fucking Zen.
It's like trying to find inner peace
while juggling flaming torches.
Like a circus performer.

Treating yourself with respect and kindness,
fight the good fight,
fight the bad fight.

My parents are no longer here,
and I often wonder if they truly existed.
Reflecting on my life,
I realized that the past is beyond comprehension,
and I still can't fully understand it at all.

One thing I know for sure:
when the time comes,
I was asked by God or angel or heaven guardian that sort,
"Are you happier in this life?"
I will stand tall and declare,
"This soul is still not particularly likable,
and I still have no clue about life, but I am fucking Zen now."

And by the way,
may I ask if there's an emergency exit
or mid-term break or something?
It is very likely I would need to return for another life if I say that.

Until then,
I will continue to cherish every experience as a privilege
and work hard to become who I am.
Who I am?
I will keep you posted as soon as possible.

Thank you.

PS.
One day, while strolling past the flower market,
a thought came to mind.
If there really is a next life,
wouldn't it be OMG to end up as plastic flowers?

小提醒

給我自己
及任何其他相關人仕的小提醒 ：

注意自己的健康。
生命只有一次。
有沒有另一次你本人應該唔會知。
繼續前進，讓生命本身有機會成為你的傑作。

這很難。好 _ 禪。
這就像一邊拋火把一邊尋找內心平靜。
活得像長期在馬戲團表演一樣。

尊重並善待自己。

我的父母已不存在，
我常常懷疑他們是否真的存在過。
回顧這段日子，
我仍然無法完全理解過去的事情。

有一件事我很確定：
當時機成熟時，上帝、天使或那一邊的接待者問我：
你離開時有沒有覺得自己幸福了一些？

我會昂首挺胸地宣布：
「這個靈魂不是特別討人喜歡，
仍然對生活不大在行。
但我現在很 _ 禪。
By the way 順便問一下，
請問有沒有緊急出口或中期休息之類？」

我知道這麼說的話，
很可能我又係需要再回來過另一 round 人生了。
或者這次是食蟻獸。

在那之前，
我將繼續珍惜每一次經歷，並努力成為我自己。
我自己是誰？
我將盡快向你通報最新情況。

謝謝。

PS.
某天經過花墟，
突然間想起如果真的有下一世，
變成塑膠花會相當大鑊。

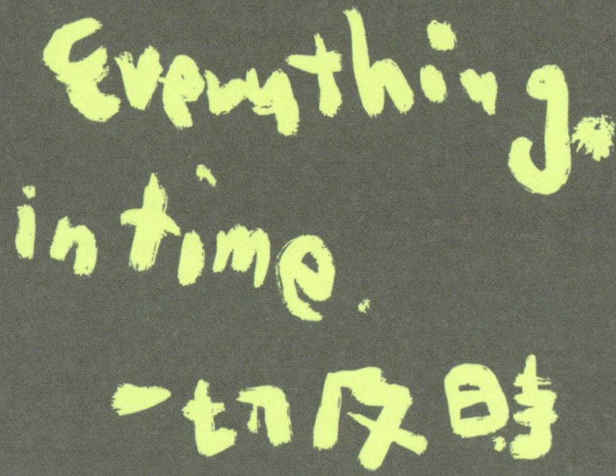

b. wing

Published & Distributed by
Syncircle Design Company Limited
Unit 12, 11/F, Eastern Harbour Centre,
28 Hoi Chak Street, Quarry Bay, Hong Kong
Tel : (852) 3748 9663
Email : info@syncircle.com

Printed by
Champion Design & Production Co. Ltd

Book Design
Lorraine Wong

Editor
Jerome To

First Edition | **June 2025**
Paperback ISBN | **978-988-71110-9-2**
Paperback $268 | **Hardback $398**

Printed & Published in Hong Kong

Open

Keaykolour Holly 120g

Body

Brisk Uncoated Smooth 150g

Antalis Pack Crush Citrus 120g

End

Keaykolour Holly 120g

Sponsored by